I0741953

One Christmas Lasts Forever

By Robert Gaines

It was late one Christmas Eve. . . cold and quiet. . . a billion stars dancing in silence. . . the falling moon dragging its shadow across the ice and snow, painting the night sky a deep and majestic blue. Christmas morning was still so far away.

Inside our home, my wife and two children were warm with sleep, but I was somewhat restless, thinking of a distant Christmas when I was a young boy . . . it would have been forty years back.

I was only eight years old that special Christmas, the same age as my oldest child is now. And I couldn't sleep that night either; calculating the distance and time it would take Santa and his team of reindeer to fly across the world.

Yes, I still believed . . . sort of . . .

Earlier that evening, while my Dad and I inspected the manger scene we had constructed on the coffee table, I had told him bluntly what had been whispered around school.

Was he listening? Dad seemed more interested in moving Baby Jesus closer to Mary and Joseph.

"Bobby," he finally said, "your friends are missing an important point. Christmas is magical . . . it's the spirit of Santa Claus that visits our home."

My dad stopped, correctly sensing that I was a bit confused. He put his giant hands to each side of my head and locked his eyes into mine.

"Always remember that we are celebrating the birth of Jesus Christ," he said. "And even though we might not see Jesus, he's here . . . as strong and real as the love that runs between you and me and our entire family. Jesus provides a bond that will always keep us together."

He kissed my forehead. "Son, the gifts from Santa Claus are a message that Jesus wants to share his birthday with each of us."

"Well Dad, I sure hope Jesus wants a new train set." My dad laughed and rubbed the top of my head.

"Bobby, I do believe it's your bedtime," he said, opening his arms for another hug. "Say good-night to everyone and don't forget to say your prayers."

Oh, I prayed . . .

A football, cowboy fort, baseball cards, and, just to be clear, a new train would be great . . . the list was quite extensive.

But that was earlier in the evening, and remember, I was only eight years old, listening for any sound that might come from the living room, wondering what would be under the Christmas tree in the morning. Maybe Santa Claus had already arrived. Maybe I could catch him – or at least his spirit – unloading his sack of toys.

Then, without a whole lot of thought, I made a daring decision . . . to sneak into our living room and check under the tree. What harm would it be?

I quietly pulled off the blanket and eased myself out of bed. Oh, it was cold . . .

I put on my robe and slippers, cautiously opening my bedroom door, an uninvited squeak blaring from a hinge. Yikes, I listened for a stir, but all was quiet.

I fought the dark hallway that night, now forty years into the past, moving ever so slowly as to not awaken my parents or sisters. It seemed like hours, each step so deliberate, so very quiet.

Finally into the living room, I crawled through a deep blue dim . . . past the fireplace and the small light from our manger scene . . . toward the shadow of our tree . . . where I discovered the tracks of an electric train . . . its engine, boxcars, and caboose.

Yes, the world was perfect . . . I so wanted to give it a test run, but wisely decided to curtail the adventure and wait for the morning.

I silently returned to my bedroom and fell fast asleep. Next morning, my parents would wake me.

"Bobby, it's Christmas," my dad proclaimed, a huge smile streaked across his face. "Let's see if Santa's been here."

I would act surprised, of course. "Wow, an electric train. Santa read my letter. This is exactly what I wanted."

I loved that train, but it wasn't even near the best gift that Christmas. My Aunt Louise and Uncle Pex were visiting from Kansas City, Uncle Billy and his family from the farm. Aunt Lillian and Uncle Don had brought my grandparents. It seemed as if all the relatives were there for Christmas dinner. The kids played, the parents talked. We laughed and sang and prayed . . . packaged every moment into happiness.

Late that night, my dad was standing by the Christmas tree, adjusting a few ornaments. Suddenly he reached into the heart of the branches and said, "Hey, what's this?"

The room was filled with family, but my dad looked directly at me.

"Bobby, I think this is for you," he said.

He put his hand on my shoulder and handed me a little metal car, hand-painted orange with bright blue wheels. Now, my father was never one to be overly sentimental, but he could pick his spots . . . and this was one of them.

"One Christmas lasts forever," he whispered to me. "Just like our family . . . it lasts forever."

So many years ago, that Christmas . . .

All the old folks are gone now, Dad almost four years. And I don't know what ever happened to my electric train or that little hand-painted orange car with the bright blue wheels.

Things change, things get old, things get lost.

With the thoughts of that childhood Christmas still blazing through my mind, I finally drifted to sleep. After all, that was four decades ago and tomorrow would be a great Christmas.

Within a deep sleep, my body twitched, my mind quickly followed . . . and I was once again wide awake. Too much excitement, I suppose, imagining the expressions of my two children as they saw their presents. Perhaps I'd sneak down the hallway one more time and check the tree.

Ever so quietly, I got out of bed and walked slowly past the children's rooms, careful not to awaken them.

Strange, but I could hear a feint sound . . . it was music, I think . . . Christmas music. Or maybe it was just the trace of a melody in my head.

"Through the years, we all will be together, if the fates allow . . ."

But now the music was louder and there seemed to be a flicker of light coming from downstairs. And laughter . . . I thought that I heard laughter.

I descended the stairs and turned the corner into the living room . . . and stood motionless, stunned.

There was my father, sitting in his chair, cleaning one of the figures from the manger scene. This absolutely could not be . . . as if I had somehow been tossed back in time . . . but, really, it was him . . . and my mother, how beautiful. My goodness, my parents were younger than me.

Suddenly, I noticed that Aunt Lillian and Grandmother Edith were putting presents under the tree while Aunt Louise talked baseball with Uncle Pex. And there was Uncle Billy, Aunt Nelda, and Grandfather Roy . . . none of them looked a day older than that Christmas long ago.

Of course, I was 48 years old, no longer a little boy . . . but this couldn't be.

"Bobby, we're so glad to see you," said Dad, putting his hand once again on my shoulder.

Mother rushed over to give me a long and wondrous hug as Aunt Louise offered a soft kiss on my cheek. And I totally forgot that this was impossible . . . just a dream gone wild. Because, you see, they were real.

Suddenly, I noticed their eyes looking beyond me.

"Daddy, who are these people?" came a voice from behind.

I turned to see my daughter, Megan, and my little boy, Robbie.

"Oh, we know these children well," said Grandmother Edith. "We visit their hearts, touch them in their dreams. And they are beautiful, Bobby . . . they are beautiful."

Without hesitation, my daughter ran and embraced her great grandmother. And then young Meggie saw my parents.

"Granddad . . . Grandmother," she screamed in delight, rushing toward two souls she had deeply loved as a small child.

Within moments, Meggie was on her grandfather's knee, Robbie being tickled and hugged by his great aunts . . . folks that he was never meant to meet in this life, on this earth.

Choked with emotion, I could barely speak. But here was my family through the ages . . . together . . . it was so strange, so wonderful.

We laughed and sang and prayed that night, told old stories, looked into each other's eyes one more time. But then it was late and the room was getting hazy. The children needed to get upstairs to their beds. All of us needed to sleep. We kissed our relatives goodnight. It was as if they had never left.

But they did . . .

By Christmas morning, my old family was gone, that distant living room once again just a memory. And my children did not say a thing.

"Just a wonderful dream," my wife said softly.

"So real," I said. "They were so real."

But now the kids were unraveling hidden treasures under the tree, Robbie gleefully wrestling with the wrapping paper.

My family was warm and happy that day. We laughed, we sang, we looked into each other's eyes . . . and held hands within our small circle for a short traditional Christmas prayer.

"Thank you, God, for this wonderful day . . . and thank you, Jesus, for sharing your birthday . . . Amen."

And very late that night, I sat down to watch my two children playing near the tree, happily consumed by a little toy. What in the world did they have? I looked closer, my mind attempting to realize exactly what I was seeing.

Meggie and Robbie were playing with a little metal car . . . hand-painted orange with bright blue wheels.

I pulled back, stunned.

"One Christmas lasts forever," my father whispered within my mind. "Just like our family . . . it lasts forever."

The End

Robert Gaines

Born into a naval family in 1945, Robert was raised in California, Rhode Island, and Virginia. Even as a child, he had an obsession for recording his stray thoughts into hundreds of notebooks.

After graduating from San Diego State, Robert became an award-winning sportswriter and columnist for the largest daily newspaper in North San Diego County, soon noted for both his humor and ability to portray the depth and compassion of his subjects.

In the early 1990s, Robert left California to become director of development communications at Bucknell University in Pennsylvania. He edited The Beauty of Bucknell (Harmony House, 2001), along with being the key writer for hundreds of university publications and several Bucknell documentaries.

One Christmas Lasts Forever is the fourth book he has had published—*The Three Mathewsons* (Hidden Shelf 2012), *The Christian Gentleman: How Christy Mathewson's Faith and Fastball Forever Changed Baseball* (Roman & Littlefield 2015), and *The Loose Chronicles* (Hidden Shelf 2017). His first novel — *The Brave Historian* — will be published by Hidden Shelf in 2020.

Sarah Harris

Sarah Harris is a digital illustrator and fine artist. She creates colorful and soft illustrations and paintings that are inspired by figure and portrait artwork, and the natural world around us. Her art education started with high school classes and she graduated from the College of Idaho with a Bachelor of Fine Arts degree.

She currently lives in Idaho with her husband, James. When she's not actively painting, she plays volleyball, enjoys backpacking and fishing, and plays video games.

Other books that Sarah has illustrated include: *The Extreme Adventures of Wrecking Rex: The BMX Race: Adventure One* by Cindy Teddy Williams, and *The Loose Chronicles: A Dog from a Distant Universe* by R.D. Gaines.

Cover design: Allison Kaukola
www.akgraphicdesigns.com

Illustrations: Sarah Harris
Social Media: @sarahharrisart

Publisher: Jessie Davis

Layout: Kerstin Stokes

Gaines, R.D.
One Christmas Lasts Forever

ISBN-13: 978-0-9996466-4-9

Printed in the United States of America